But God Remembered

But God Remembered

STORIES OF WOMEN

FROM CREATION TO THE

PROMISED LAND

Sandy Eisenberg Sasso

ILLUSTRATED BY BETHANNE ANDERSEN

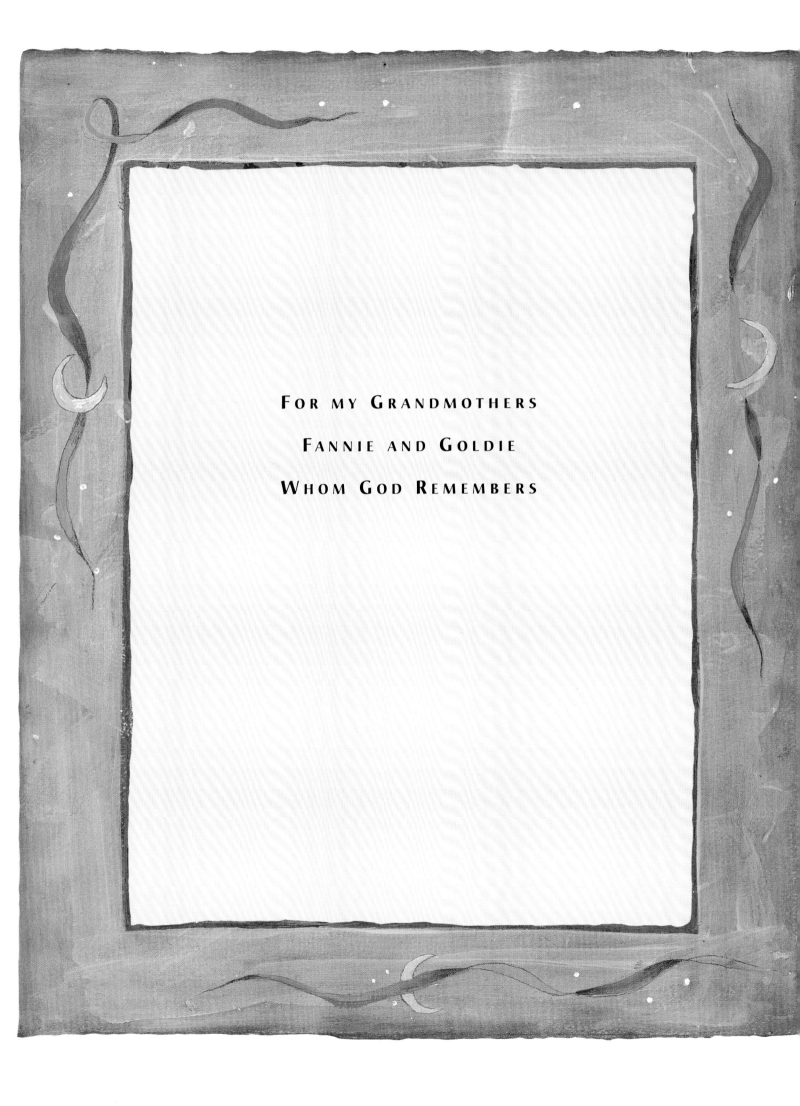

FOR MY GRANDMOTHERS

FANNIE AND GOLDIE

WHOM GOD REMEMBERS

Before God created man and woman, God wanted to create Memory and Forgetfulness. But the angels protested.

The Angel of Song said, "Do not create Forgetfulness. People will forget the songs of their ancestors."

The Angel of Stories said, "If you create Forgetfulness, man and woman will forget many good stories."

The Angel of Names said, "Forget songs? Forget stories? They will not even remember each other's names."

God listened to the complaints of the angels. And God asked the angels what kinds of things they remembered.

At first, the angels remembered what it was like before the world was formed. Then as the angels talked about the time before time existed, they recalled moments when they did not always agree.

One angel yelled at another, "I remember when your fiery sword burned the hem of my robe!"

"And I remember when you knocked me down and tore a hole in my wing," screamed another.

As the angels remembered everything that ever happened, their voices grew louder and louder and louder until the heavens thundered.

God said, "FORGET IT!"

And there was Forgetfulness.

All at once the angels forgot why they were angry at each other and their voices became angelic again. And God saw that it was good.

God said, "There are some things people will need to forget."

The angels objected. "People will forget what they should remember."

God said, "I will remember all the important things. I will plant the seeds of remembrance in the soul of My people."

And so it was that over time people forgot many of the songs, stories and names of their ancestors.

But God remembered.

WHAT IS
Midrash?

Many stories in the Bible are well known, like those of Abraham and Isaac, Moses on Mount Sinai, David and Goliath. But other stories are only brief sketches and seem incomplete. We often wonder about what has been left out. When we read the Bible, we imagine what else the women and men in a story might have thought, said or done.

Suppose you are reading the biblical story about Lot's wife turning back to see the destruction of Sodom and Gomorrah, and about her becoming a pillar of salt. You wonder why she turned around, and why she became a pillar of salt. Suppose you say she turned around out of compassion for those left behind, and the pillar of salt was from her tears. In adding this explanation, you would be creating a type of story which in Hebrew is called *midrash*. Many such stories were told by our ancestors to enrich the stories of the Bible. In time, some of these were written down, and then they were read again and again until they began to feel very old, as if they were always part of tradition.

This is a book of *midrash*: four stories about women from biblical and ancient times who are not well known. Almost no one remembers them, not even their names. These stories imagine and remember.

LILITH,
THE FIRST WOMAN

"God created man and woman in the Divine image.
In God's image they were created;
male and female God created them."

(GENESIS 1:27)

IN THE BEGINNING WHEN GOD CREATED MAN AND WOMAN, God called the first man Adam and the first woman, God called Lilith. The first man and first woman were both created from the same earth and God's breath made them come alive. In the beginning, they shared everything.

God planted a garden in Eden and placed Adam and Lilith there to till it and tend it together. Adam and Lilith loved the garden that God had made, and they loved each other.

Lilith would climb the trees to gather pomegranates. Adam and Lilith loved to play catch with the gold-red fruit that seemed to come together on the bottom in a kiss. When they were tired of playing, Lilith would take the pomegranates and split them open. Adam would scoop out the juicy seeds. Then Adam and Lilith would sit by the river that flowed through the garden and suck on the pomegranate seeds together.

Sometimes Adam would gather sweet oranges and peel them for Lilith, and Lilith would squeeze the oranges in her hands to make juice. She would hold hands with Adam, and they would laugh when their hands stuck together.

The garden where Adam and Lilith lived was rich with colors and filled with sounds. But the garden was very large, and they could not possibly see all its beauty from where they stood on the ground.

Sometimes Adam would kneel down and Lilith would climb on his shoulders, reach to the tallest tree and look out and describe all that she saw. She told of big beautiful birds who spread a fan of colors and yellow animals with black spots and a long neck. And Lilith called the birds with a fan of colors peacocks, and the long-necked creatures she called giraffes.

Sometimes Lilith would kneel down, and Adam would climb on her shoulders, reach to the tallest tree and look out and describe all that he saw. He told of big golden animals with large hairy manes and small gray animals with bushy tails that stood straight up in the air. And Adam called the golden animals lions, and the bushy-tailed creatures he called squirrels.

Now Adam and Lilith loved giving names to all the animals, and they loved each other. And God saw all that was going on in the garden, and God found it very good.

Then one day, Adam grew tired of letting Lilith climb on his shoulders to look out over the garden. "Lilith, I have a new idea." Adam's voice quivered, but he went right on speaking. "I think only one of us should name the animals, and I should be the one. In return, I will go after the pomegranates and split them open and squeeze all the oranges."

Lilith was silent for a long time. "Adam," she finally said, "I do not like your new idea. I love to fetch the pomegranates and split them open. I like the sticky feeling when I squeeze the oranges. But most of all, I enjoy climbing on your shoulders to reach the tallest tree, look out over the garden and name the animals."

"Lilith, we are different. We should do different things," said Adam, folding his arms across his chest. "I won't let you climb on my shoulders anymore. Now I want to be the only one to name the creatures in the garden."

Lilith said, "Well, then I won't let you climb on my shoulders either. But we both should name the animals."

Adam said, "But my names are better than your names!"

Lilith said, "My names are better!"

And Adam said, "Are not!"

And Lilith said, "Are so!"

Adam and Lilith argued, and their voices became louder and louder. And God heard Adam and Lilith and all that was going on in the garden, and God did not find it very good at all.

Lilith would not talk to Adam. She walked a whole day's journey to another part of the garden and ate her oranges alone.

Adam would not go after Lilith. He stayed where he was and ate his pomegranates by himself.

Until finally, Adam was so lonely, he said to God, "Creator of the world, bring Lilith back to me. Make her return."

And God answered, "This is something only you can do."

But Adam refused.

Lilith said to God, "Creator of man and woman, make Adam come back to me. Make things between Adam and me as they were in the beginning."

And God answered, "This is something only you can do."

But Lilith refused.

God saw Adam and Lilith and how very lonely they were. And God was sad for the first man and the first woman.

After a while, Adam found comfort with a new companion named Eve. Adam called his new companion the *first* woman, because he wanted to forget Lilith. In the course of time, people forgot Lilith's story and how man and woman were once equal.

But God remembered Lilith, and God named the night after her. That is why in Hebrew the night is called *laila*. Some say Lilith stretches the night sky over all God's creation. She spreads a canopy of stars to light the dark and calls each star by name.

A PSALM OF SERACH

*...e are the names of the Israelites,
...is descendants who came to Egypt....
Asher's sons...
...and their sister Serach."*

(GENESIS 46:8-17)

...FAMINE IN CANAAN, THERE WAS A ...over four hundred years. She always carried her harp and ...t her long life, she grew in wisdom, but her voice remained

...ob's sons went down to Egypt to find food for their family, they returned with wagons overflowing with grain, and they carried surprising news. Their brother Joseph was Prime Minister of Egypt! Joseph had been Jacob's favorite son, and his brothers had been jealous of him. They had sold him into slavery, and then told Jacob that Joseph had been torn apart by an animal. But Joseph was neither dead nor a slave.

13

Not one of the eleven brothers would tell Jacob that Joseph was alive. Not one would admit to his act of jealousy and say he had lied. But if they did not tell Jacob about Joseph, they could never convince him to go with them to Egypt where food was plentiful and the land was good. They only brought back enough grain to last a few weeks. Jacob would have to be told.

As the brothers unloaded their wagons and argued over who would tell Jacob, they heard singing and the sounds of a harp coming from a nearby tent. For a moment, they relaxed in the cradle of the song.

Asher, one of the brothers, said, "The music comes from my daughter Serach. God has blessed her with grace and wisdom and has given her the gifts of song and story."

And it was so. The voice of Serach softened the harshness of the famine. Children often followed her on her walks and listened to her sing of their ancestors. She sang of Abraham and Isaac, Sarah and Rebekkah. She spoke of Hagar, Ishmael and Esau. She sang of Jacob and his sons and Dinah, his daughter. All the people of Israel listened to the songs of Serach.

When Serach finished her song and her playing upon the harp, Asher thought of a plan. "Serach is the one to tell Jacob that his son Joseph still lives. Her song brings understanding, and her music quiets the troubled heart."

All the brothers agreed. Asher went to Serach's tent and pleaded with her to tell their story. "My daughter, my beloved Serach, we need your help. We have just returned from Egypt where there is food in abundance. The man who sits by Pharaoh's side, his Prime Minister, is our brother Joseph! Jacob must know his son lives. Then he will lead us all to Egypt, to sweet water and grain, fresh fish and melons. Jacob is old and his heart is broken. We tricked our father once, and we cannot speak to him about Joseph again. Our words are clumsy, old lies tie our tongues. But your voice, Serach, is not like ours. Be our voice before Jacob."

Serach was silent for a long time. She loved her father who had honored her by teaching her the wisdom of the ancestors. Other daughters were given no such knowledge. She knew the ancient stories by heart and wrote words to sing and music to play upon the strings of her harp. Could she find the words to tell her grandfather Jacob about Joseph's new life? Could she calm his soul in the rhythms of her song? What if she failed? The children of Israel were often hungry. Without Jacob, they would not go down to Egypt.

Serach decided to write a song for her grandfather. The next morning, she took her harp and went to his tent. Serach sat down

before her grandfather and began to play a sweet melody. She called it *A Psalm of Serach, for Jacob. On the harp.*

Once your sons handed you Joseph's bloody coat.
You wept and mourned; you no longer had hope.
But a miracle has happened. It's almost a dream.
Come closer, grandfather, hear the words that I sing.

When your sons went to visit Egypt land,
They bowed and kissed a ruler's fair hand.
They did not know his face, nor recognize his voice.
But the words he spoke gave them reason to rejoice.
"From Egypt's storehouse I have grain I can give.
I am Joseph, your brother. Does our father still live?"

Your sons were afraid, sorry and ashamed.
For what happened to Joseph, they accepted the blame.
Joseph said, "It was God who brought me to this place.
Now all that I wish is to see my father's face."

What your sons once said of Joseph's end was not true.
Joseph's forgiven them. They pray you'll forgive them too.
Go down to Egypt. Don't wait too long.
Unite our family. Fulfill the promise of this song.

Serach sang the melody over and over again. The song gave Jacob much joy and delight. All the years he was separated from Joseph, Jacob grieved, but Serach's song lifted his spirits and he felt happiness once again. He knew Serach spoke the truth. Her song gave him new strength, and her words gave his heart the ability to forgive.

When she finished her song, Jacob embraced Serach and blessed her. "May your songs and stories live forever among our people."

Serach went down to Egypt with Jacob and his sons and daughter, and she became the head of a large family. No one really knows what happened to her, but four hundred years later it was said

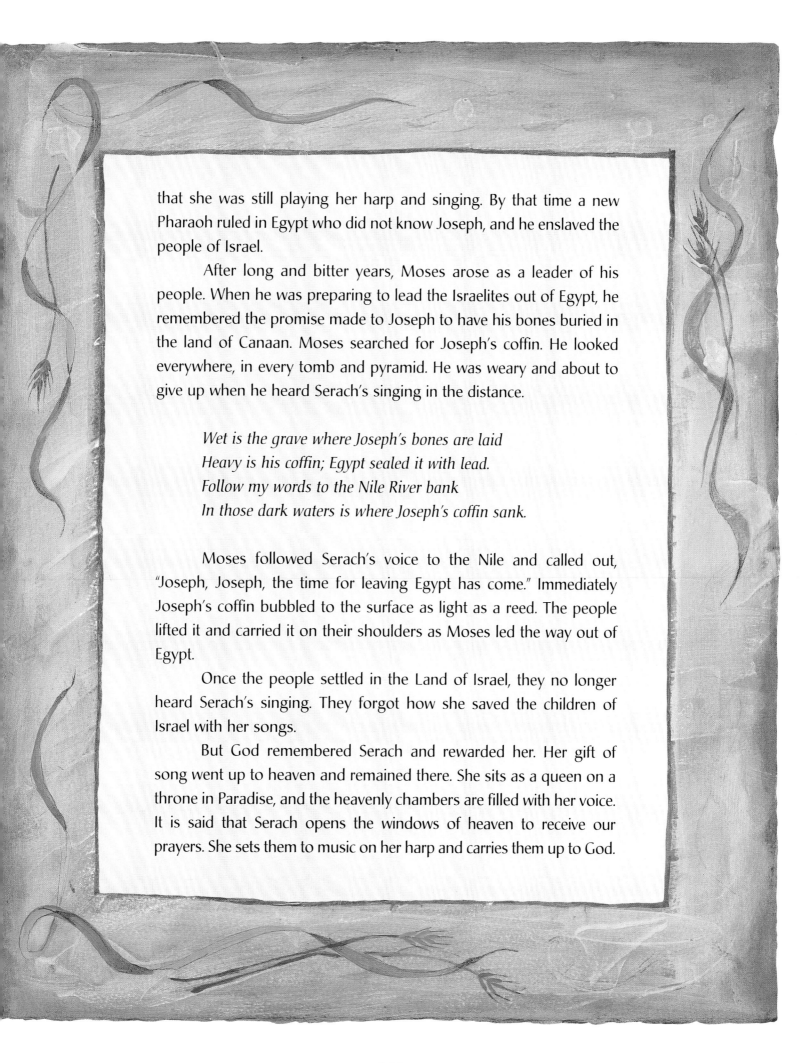

that she was still playing her harp and singing. By that time a new Pharaoh ruled in Egypt who did not know Joseph, and he enslaved the people of Israel.

After long and bitter years, Moses arose as a leader of his people. When he was preparing to lead the Israelites out of Egypt, he remembered the promise made to Joseph to have his bones buried in the land of Canaan. Moses searched for Joseph's coffin. He looked everywhere, in every tomb and pyramid. He was weary and about to give up when he heard Serach's singing in the distance.

Wet is the grave where Joseph's bones are laid
Heavy is his coffin; Egypt sealed it with lead.
Follow my words to the Nile River bank
In those dark waters is where Joseph's coffin sank.

Moses followed Serach's voice to the Nile and called out, "Joseph, Joseph, the time for leaving Egypt has come." Immediately Joseph's coffin bubbled to the surface as light as a reed. The people lifted it and carried it on their shoulders as Moses led the way out of Egypt.

Once the people settled in the Land of Israel, they no longer heard Serach's singing. They forgot how she saved the children of Israel with her songs.

But God remembered Serach and rewarded her. Her gift of song went up to heaven and remained there. She sits as a queen on a throne in Paradise, and the heavenly chambers are filled with her voice. It is said that Serach opens the windows of heaven to receive our prayers. She sets them to music on her harp and carries them up to God.

BITYAH, DAUGHTER OF GOD

"When the child grew up, she brought him to
Pharaoh's daughter who made him her son.
She named him Moses, explaining
I drew him out of the water."

(EXODUS 2:10)

THE PHARAOH HAD A DAUGHTER NAMED MEROE WHO LOVED
to bathe in the cool waters of the Nile. Her handmaids always joined her and stood by her side as she washed. One day as Meroe knelt down and scooped up water to splash on her face, she saw a little basket floating among the reeds. She knew it held a Hebrew child placed there to escape her father's terrible decree.

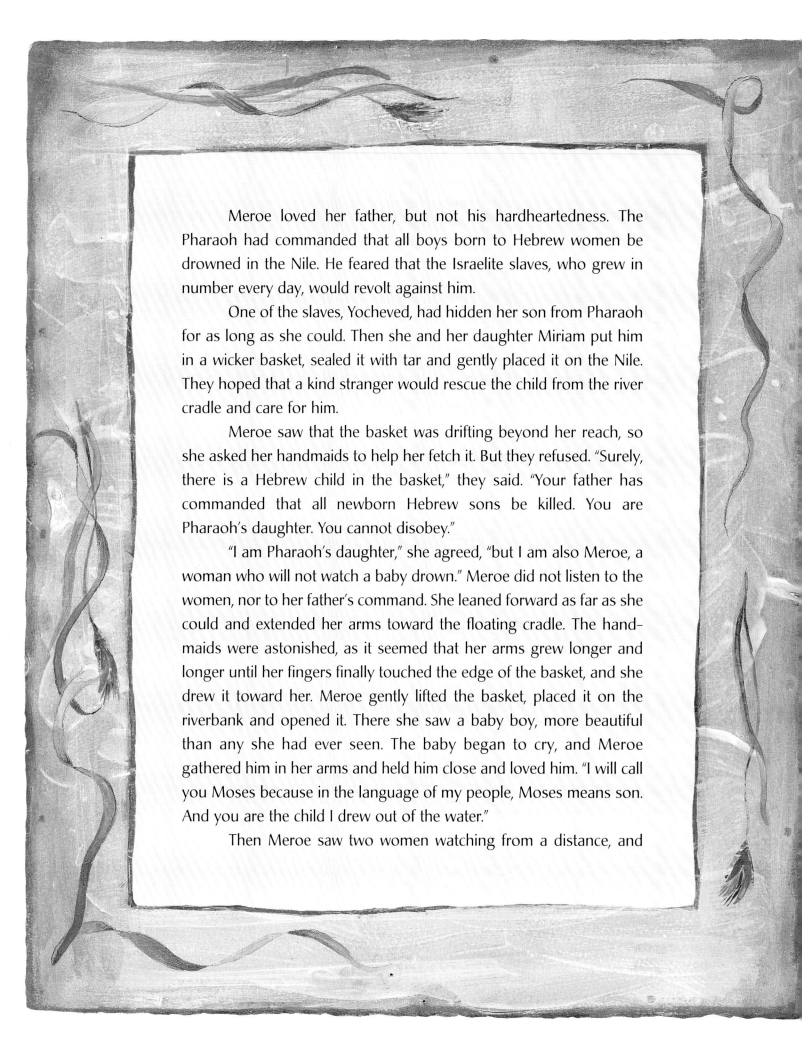

Meroe loved her father, but not his hardheartedness. The Pharaoh had commanded that all boys born to Hebrew women be drowned in the Nile. He feared that the Israelite slaves, who grew in number every day, would revolt against him.

One of the slaves, Yocheved, had hidden her son from Pharaoh for as long as she could. Then she and her daughter Miriam put him in a wicker basket, sealed it with tar and gently placed it on the Nile. They hoped that a kind stranger would rescue the child from the river cradle and care for him.

Meroe saw that the basket was drifting beyond her reach, so she asked her handmaids to help her fetch it. But they refused. "Surely, there is a Hebrew child in the basket," they said. "Your father has commanded that all newborn Hebrew sons be killed. You are Pharaoh's daughter. You cannot disobey."

"I am Pharaoh's daughter," she agreed, "but I am also Meroe, a woman who will not watch a baby drown." Meroe did not listen to the women, nor to her father's command. She leaned forward as far as she could and extended her arms toward the floating cradle. The hand-maids were astonished, as it seemed that her arms grew longer and longer until her fingers finally touched the edge of the basket, and she drew it toward her. Meroe gently lifted the basket, placed it on the riverbank and opened it. There she saw a baby boy, more beautiful than any she had ever seen. The baby began to cry, and Meroe gathered him in her arms and held him close and loved him. "I will call you Moses because in the language of my people, Moses means son. And you are the child I drew out of the water."

Then Meroe saw two women watching from a distance, and

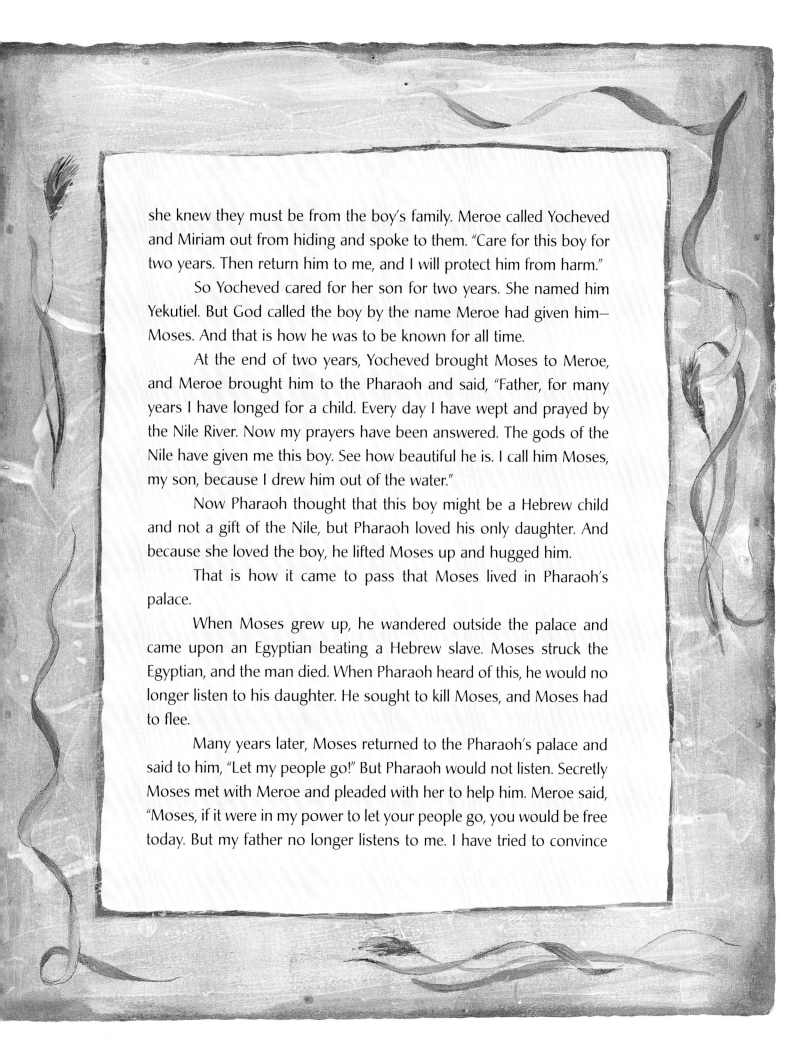

she knew they must be from the boy's family. Meroe called Yocheved and Miriam out from hiding and spoke to them. "Care for this boy for two years. Then return him to me, and I will protect him from harm."

So Yocheved cared for her son for two years. She named him Yekutiel. But God called the boy by the name Meroe had given him—Moses. And that is how he was to be known for all time.

At the end of two years, Yocheved brought Moses to Meroe, and Meroe brought him to the Pharaoh and said, "Father, for many years I have longed for a child. Every day I have wept and prayed by the Nile River. Now my prayers have been answered. The gods of the Nile have given me this boy. See how beautiful he is. I call him Moses, my son, because I drew him out of the water."

Now Pharaoh thought that this boy might be a Hebrew child and not a gift of the Nile, but Pharaoh loved his only daughter. And because she loved the boy, he lifted Moses up and hugged him.

That is how it came to pass that Moses lived in Pharaoh's palace.

When Moses grew up, he wandered outside the palace and came upon an Egyptian beating a Hebrew slave. Moses struck the Egyptian, and the man died. When Pharaoh heard of this, he would no longer listen to his daughter. He sought to kill Moses, and Moses had to flee.

Many years later, Moses returned to the Pharaoh's palace and said to him, "Let my people go!" But Pharaoh would not listen. Secretly Moses met with Meroe and pleaded with her to help him. Meroe said, "Moses, if it were in my power to let your people go, you would be free today. But my father no longer listens to me. I have tried to convince him to allow your people to leave Egypt. But as soon as he agrees, he changes his mind. Be careful, Moses. My father is angry, and his heart is hard. For you, I will speak with him again. And when the time comes for you to go out of Egypt, remember me."

Moses promised Meroe that no matter what plagues and hardships would befall her people, no harm would come to her. Nine times Pharaoh agreed to let Israel go. Nine times he changed his mind and brought disaster upon his people. Then a final terrible plague spread over all of Egypt, and Pharaoh let the people of Israel go.

It was in the middle of the night when Moses went to see Meroe one last time. "Come with us out of Egypt," Moses pleaded.

"I cannot go with you," she said. "I belong here." Meroe embraced Moses for a long time, and then she tore herself away. "Do not delay," she urged, "or my father will change his mind again." She swallowed hard and held back tears. "Goodbye, Moses, and may the God of freedom bless you."

Moses said, "Because you loved a stranger as your son, I will teach my people to care for the stranger, and so they will remember you. Peace to you, Meroe, and may the God of all people bless you."

Meroe was pleased for Moses, but sad for her people. Meroe watched Moses walk away until she could no longer see him in the distance. Then she turned back to comfort her father.

Moses led Israel through the sea to freedom. The people told stories about Meroe and about how she had saved Moses, a stranger, and loved him. Moses taught, "You shall not oppress the stranger, for you know the heart of the stranger, having yourselves been strangers in the land of Egypt." But after awhile, the people forgot the woman who had rescued Moses from the Nile and no longer knew her name or told her story.

But God remembered Meroe and blessed her. "As you saved Moses and called him your son even though he was not your son, so your name will no longer be Meroe but Bityah, which means daughter of God."

It is said that Bityah, daughter of God, sits at the entrance to one of the gates of Paradise, and whenever a stranger is welcomed somewhere in the world, it is Bityah who bestows God's blessing.

THE DAUGHTERS OF Z

"The daughters of Zelophehad...came forward....
The names of the daughters were
Mahlah, Noa, Hoglah, Milcah and Tirzah."

(NUMBERS 27:1)

AFTER FORTY LONG YEARS OF WANDERING IN THE DESERT, the people of Israel prepared to enter the Promised Land. Everyone was to have a piece of the land—everyone, that is, except the women. That was the law and no one questioned the law—no one, that is, except the daughters of Zelophehad. Their names were Mahlah, Noa, Hoglah, Milcah and Tirzah. People affectionately called them the daughters of Z.

Each evening Mahlah and Noa set up their tent. Hoglah and Milcah took it down again

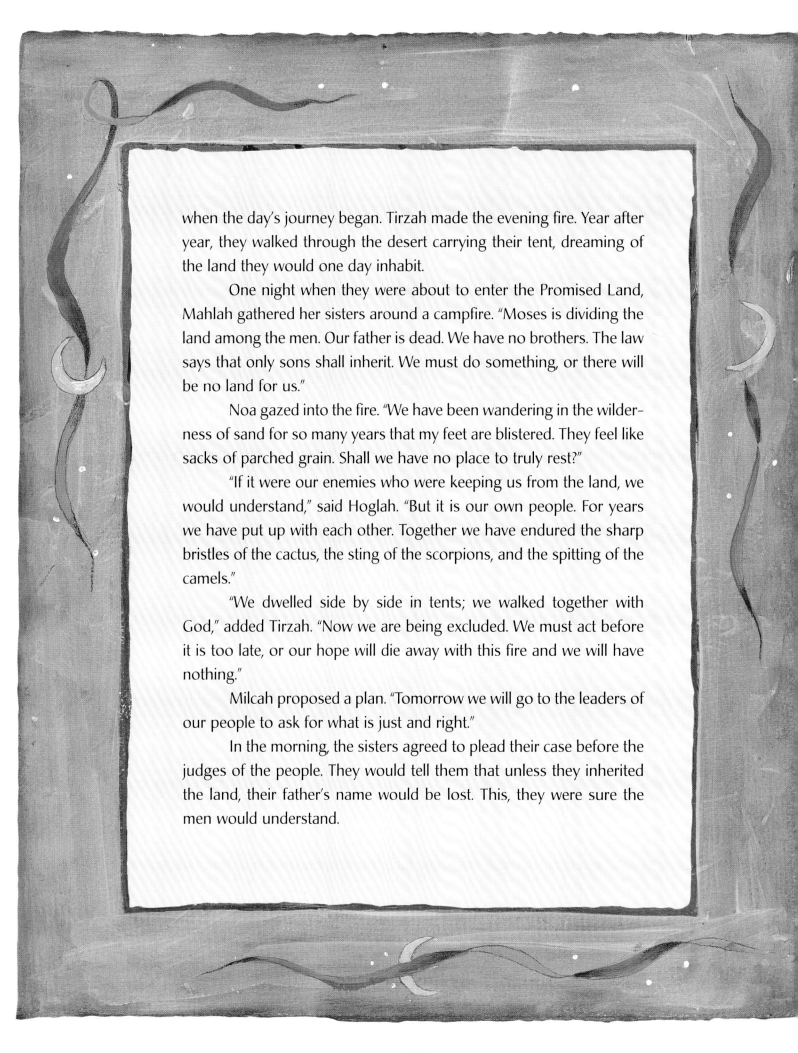

when the day's journey began. Tirzah made the evening fire. Year after year, they walked through the desert carrying their tent, dreaming of the land they would one day inhabit.

One night when they were about to enter the Promised Land, Mahlah gathered her sisters around a campfire. "Moses is dividing the land among the men. Our father is dead. We have no brothers. The law says that only sons shall inherit. We must do something, or there will be no land for us."

Noa gazed into the fire. "We have been wandering in the wilderness of sand for so many years that my feet are blistered. They feel like sacks of parched grain. Shall we have no place to truly rest?"

"If it were our enemies who were keeping us from the land, we would understand," said Hoglah. "But it is our own people. For years we have put up with each other. Together we have endured the sharp bristles of the cactus, the sting of the scorpions, and the spitting of the camels."

"We dwelled side by side in tents; we walked together with God," added Tirzah. "Now we are being excluded. We must act before it is too late, or our hope will die away with this fire and we will have nothing."

Milcah proposed a plan. "Tomorrow we will go to the leaders of our people to ask for what is just and right."

In the morning, the sisters agreed to plead their case before the judges of the people. They would tell them that unless they inherited the land, their father's name would be lost. This, they were sure the men would understand.

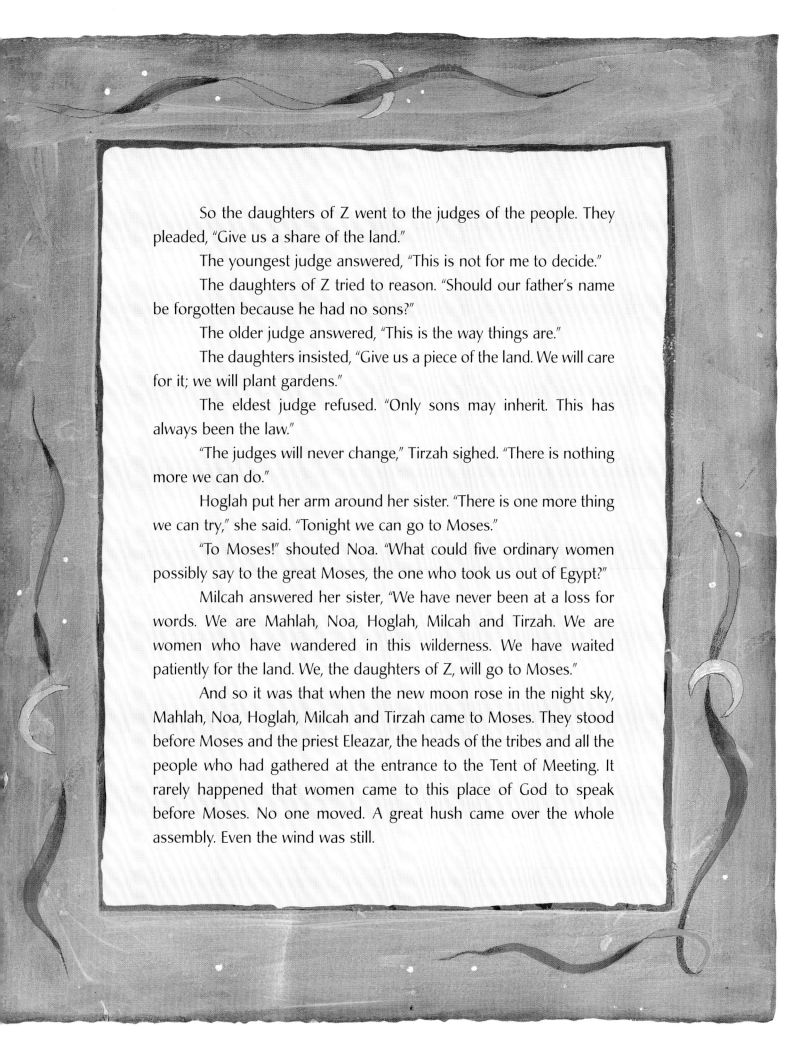

So the daughters of Z went to the judges of the people. They pleaded, "Give us a share of the land."

The youngest judge answered, "This is not for me to decide."

The daughters of Z tried to reason. "Should our father's name be forgotten because he had no sons?"

The older judge answered, "This is the way things are."

The daughters insisted, "Give us a piece of the land. We will care for it; we will plant gardens."

The eldest judge refused. "Only sons may inherit. This has always been the law."

"The judges will never change," Tirzah sighed. "There is nothing more we can do."

Hoglah put her arm around her sister. "There is one more thing we can try," she said. "Tonight we can go to Moses."

"To Moses!" shouted Noa. "What could five ordinary women possibly say to the great Moses, the one who took us out of Egypt?"

Milcah answered her sister, "We have never been at a loss for words. We are Mahlah, Noa, Hoglah, Milcah and Tirzah. We are women who have wandered in this wilderness. We have waited patiently for the land. We, the daughters of Z, will go to Moses."

And so it was that when the new moon rose in the night sky, Mahlah, Noa, Hoglah, Milcah and Tirzah came to Moses. They stood before Moses and the priest Eleazar, the heads of the tribes and all the people who had gathered at the entrance to the Tent of Meeting. It rarely happened that women came to this place of God to speak before Moses. No one moved. A great hush came over the whole assembly. Even the wind was still.

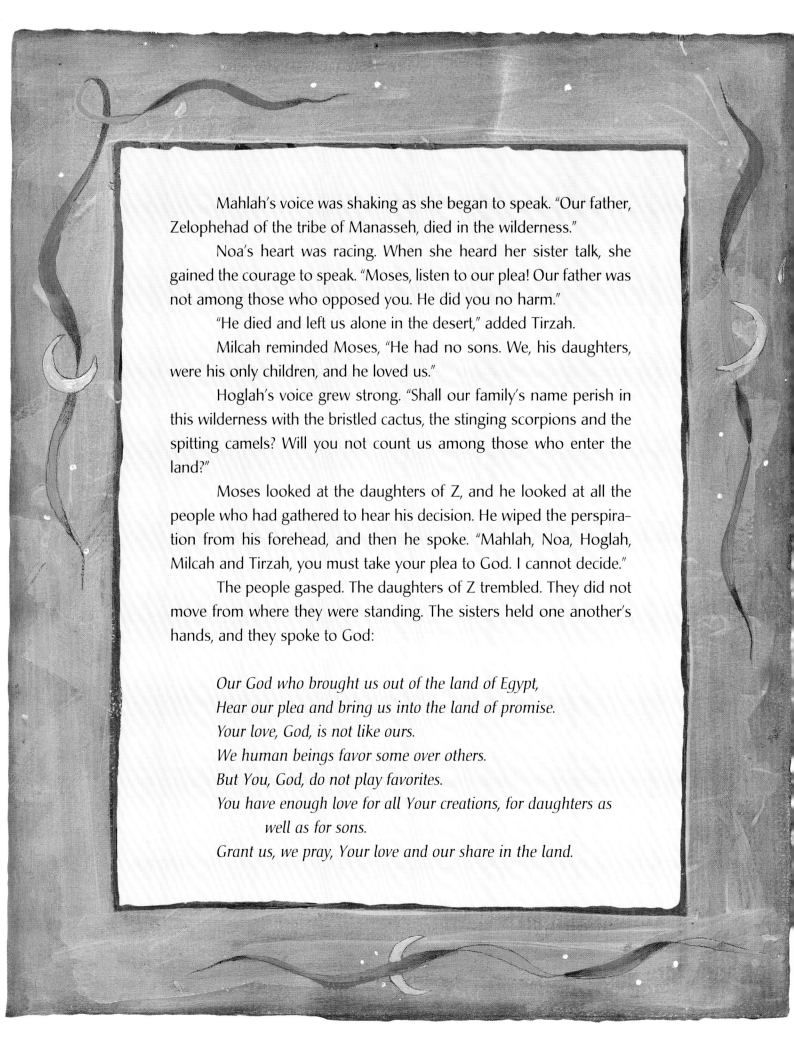

Mahlah's voice was shaking as she began to speak. "Our father, Zelophehad of the tribe of Manasseh, died in the wilderness."

Noa's heart was racing. When she heard her sister talk, she gained the courage to speak. "Moses, listen to our plea! Our father was not among those who opposed you. He did you no harm."

"He died and left us alone in the desert," added Tirzah.

Milcah reminded Moses, "He had no sons. We, his daughters, were his only children, and he loved us."

Hoglah's voice grew strong. "Shall our family's name perish in this wilderness with the bristled cactus, the stinging scorpions and the spitting camels? Will you not count us among those who enter the land?"

Moses looked at the daughters of Z, and he looked at all the people who had gathered to hear his decision. He wiped the perspiration from his forehead, and then he spoke. "Mahlah, Noa, Hoglah, Milcah and Tirzah, you must take your plea to God. I cannot decide."

The people gasped. The daughters of Z trembled. They did not move from where they were standing. The sisters held one another's hands, and they spoke to God:

Our God who brought us out of the land of Egypt,
Hear our plea and bring us into the land of promise.
Your love, God, is not like ours.
We human beings favor some over others.
But You, God, do not play favorites.
You have enough love for all Your creations, for daughters as
*   well as for sons.*
Grant us, we pray, Your love and our share in the land.

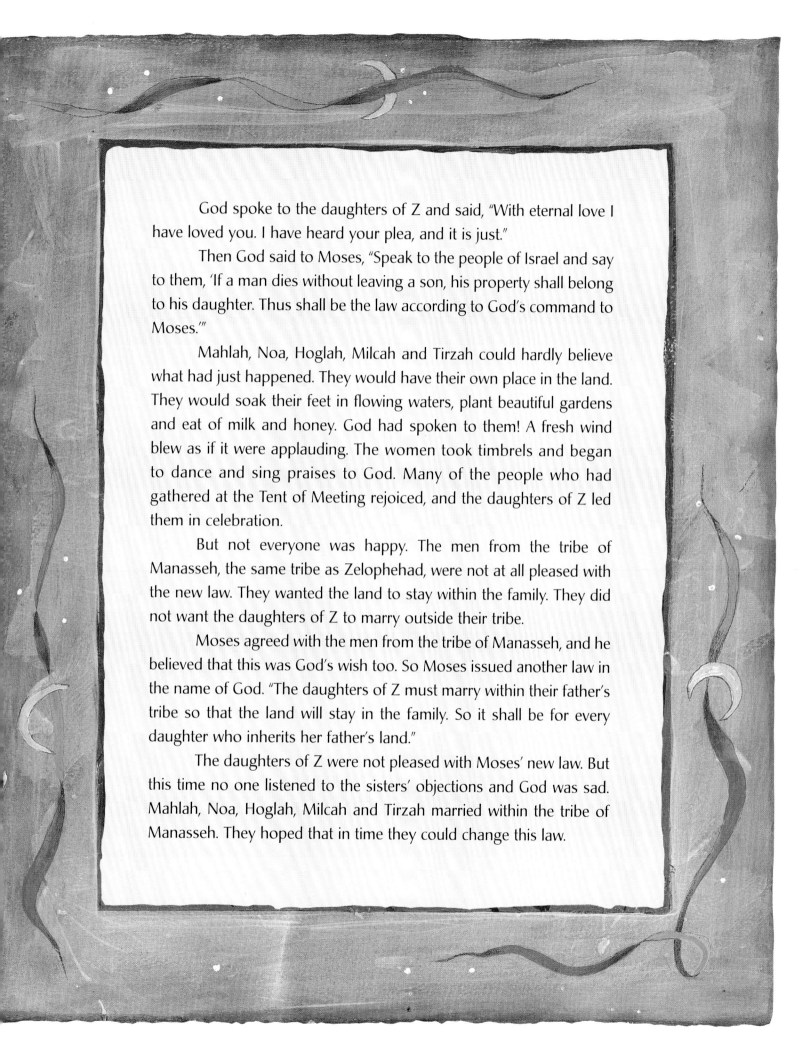

God spoke to the daughters of Z and said, "With eternal love I have loved you. I have heard your plea, and it is just."

Then God said to Moses, "Speak to the people of Israel and say to them, 'If a man dies without leaving a son, his property shall belong to his daughter. Thus shall be the law according to God's command to Moses.'"

Mahlah, Noa, Hoglah, Milcah and Tirzah could hardly believe what had just happened. They would have their own place in the land. They would soak their feet in flowing waters, plant beautiful gardens and eat of milk and honey. God had spoken to them! A fresh wind blew as if it were applauding. The women took timbrels and began to dance and sing praises to God. Many of the people who had gathered at the Tent of Meeting rejoiced, and the daughters of Z led them in celebration.

But not everyone was happy. The men from the tribe of Manasseh, the same tribe as Zelophehad, were not at all pleased with the new law. They wanted the land to stay within the family. They did not want the daughters of Z to marry outside their tribe.

Moses agreed with the men from the tribe of Manasseh, and he believed that this was God's wish too. So Moses issued another law in the name of God. "The daughters of Z must marry within their father's tribe so that the land will stay in the family. So it shall be for every daughter who inherits her father's land."

The daughters of Z were not pleased with Moses' new law. But this time no one listened to the sisters' objections and God was sad. Mahlah, Noa, Hoglah, Milcah and Tirzah married within the tribe of Manasseh. They hoped that in time they could change this law.

But after the people had settled in the land of Israel, they forgot about Mahlah, Noa, Hoglah, Milcah and Tirzah. They forgot how the daughters of Z had spoken to God and helped make a new law for all the people.

But God remembered the daughters of Z, their courage and their prayer. It is said that their spirit returns to the earth each month when the moon is new, and God's love blesses us all.

Acknowledgments

I am indebted to a rich rabbinic midrashic tradition which has inspired and helped to shape these stories. A special word of thanks to Amy Gottlieb for her caring hand and insightful eye which skillfully edited these pages. My thanks also to the wonderful people at Jewish Lights: Stuart Matlins, Sandra Korinchak, and Kimberly Lawrence, whose artistry and love of bookmaking grace this work. I am grateful to the women of the Beth-El Zedeck Sisterhood Study Group who encouraged me to write down the stories we studied together and to the children who taught me the joy of storytelling. My gratitude to Shirley Gilson, Anne Jones, and Bonnie Shute for their helpful reading of the manuscript and to Mary K. Cauley for her patient typing of the stories. My deepest thanks to my husband, Dennis, and my children, David and Debora, for their gifts of words and song, humor and love. These stories are for you; pass them on.

But God Remembered:
Stories of Women from Creation to the Promised Land

First Quality Paperback Printing 2008
Third Hardcover Printing 2000
Second Hardcover Printing 1995
First Hardcover Printing 1995
Text copyright © 1995 by Sandy Eisenberg Sasso
Illustrations © 1995 by Jewish Lights Publishing

For information regarding permission to reprint material from this book, please mail or fax your request in writing to Jewish Lights Publishing, Permissions Department, at the address / fax number listed below, or e-mail your request to permissions@jewishlights.com.

LIBRARY OF CONGRESS CATALOGING-IN-PUBLICATION DATA

Sasso, Sandy Eisenberg.
But God remembered : stories of women from creation to the promised land / by Sandy Eisenberg Sasso ; illustrated by Bethanne Andersen.
p.   cm.
Summary: Here are stories that might have happened, about four women of biblical tradition.
ISBN-13: 978-1-879045-43-9 (hardcover)
ISBN-10: 1-879045-43-5 (hardcover)
1. Women in the Bible—Juvenile literature. [1.Women in the Bible. 2. Midrash.] I. Andersen, Bethanne. 1954-   ill.
II. Title.
BS575.S33 1995   95-3591
221.9′22′082—dc20   CIP
                               AC
ISBN-13: 978-1-58023-372-9 (quality pbk.)
ISBN-10: 1-58023-372-4 (quality pbk.)

First Paperback Edition
10 9 8 7 6 5 4 3 2 1

Manufactured in China
Book and cover design by Karen Savary

For People of All Faiths, All Backgrounds

JEWISH LIGHTS Publishing
Sunset Farm Offices, Route 4, P.O. Box 237
Woodstock, VT 05091
Tel: (802) 457-4000
Fax: (802) 457-4004

www.jewishlights.com